Fabulous Five-Minute Stories

Everybody's Helper

Written by Stephanie Marbury

Illustrated by Jamie Smith

Reader's Digest Young Families

Winter was coming. A chilly breeze rustled the trees and sent showers of colorful leaves to the ground. Jack Rabbit was hurrying off into the forest.

"Why aren't you working on building your winter home, Jack?" asked his friend Benny. "They say it's going to be the coldest winter in years."

"The Beavers want me to baby-sit now," called Jack over his shoulder. "I'll get to building it later today."

"Oh, Jack, thanks so much for helping us out on such short notice!" said Mrs. Beaver when Jack arrived.

"No problem," said Jack cheerfully. "Little Beaver and I plan to have a lot of fun while you're both in town."

For much of the afternoon, Jack and Little Beaver read books, drew pictures, and played hide-and-seek.

As soon as the Beavers returned, Jack headed over to visit his friend Bill Badger. "Hello, Bill!" called Jack. "Everything all right with you? You don't look very happy."

Bill groaned and looked weakly at Jack. "I ate too many cherries," he said. "My stomach hurts."

Jack fanned his friend with a broad leaf and then made him a cup of tea.

"Thanks, Jack," said Bill. "You're such a great help! I feel better already. In fact, I'm a bit hungry. Would you see if there are any cherries left in my cupboard?"

As Jack hurried home, he looked up at the darkening sky. "I had better get started on my house," he said to himself. "It looks like snow will be coming soon."

But suddenly he heard a chittering noise above his head.

"Oh, Jack, thank goodness it's you!" called Cheryl Squirrel. "Please come in and help me with little Earl. I told him a joke, and he laughed so hard he fell out of the tree."

Earl did look a bit dazed. And his chittering was not making much sense, at least according to Cheryl. So Jack examined Earl's sore head and wrapped it in a tidy bandage. Then he gently helped him to his feet and put him to bed.

As Jack was leaving Cheryl's house, Sadie Spider dropped down from a tree branch and dangled daintily from her silken thread.

"Sorry to bother you at this busy time of year, Jack," she said. "But the wind just blew a very large leaf on my web. Would you please help me remove it?"

Always happy to help, Jack climbed onto a high rock to reach Sadie's web. Very carefully, so as not to tear its fine silk threads, he plucked off the leaf.

"Thank you, Jack," said Sadie, waggling a long leg at him. "I knew I could count on you."

As Jack passed the pond, Grandma Duck quacked for help. "Jack!" she quacked. "Can you help me with Zack?"

A duckling was stuck between two rocks. He had tried to swim between them but couldn't make it through.

Jack hurried over and carefully wiggled and pushed the rocks until Zack was finally set free.

"Thank you, Jack!" the Duck Family all quacked.

Continuing on his way, Jack came upon the Sparrow Family, whose tree was in danger of falling down. He helped them move their nest to a different tree. Then he helped Wilma Woodpecker, who lived nearby, put her wing in a sling.

"You are so helpful!" they all called after him. "Thank you, Jack!"

By the time Jack reached his burrow, darkness was setting in and a few snowflakes were beginning to fall. An icy wind had sprung up and dry leaves danced around his feet.

"Where have you been?" asked Benny. "Our winter homes are all finished and you haven't even started yours! It's going to be a cold night, my friend."

Jack sighed and looked around for a place to rest. He dug out a little hollow in the hillside and fell into a weary sleep.

Jack was awakened early the next morning by whispers and rustlings in the leaves. He was cold and stiff, but he opened his eyes wide.

There were his friends, building a house — a big house. Bill Badger had finished digging the basement, and Mr. and Mrs. Beaver were hammering away at the frame. Earl Squirrel was pushing a cart filled with some of the food Cheryl had been storing up. Wilma Woodpecker and the Sparrows were making a roof from twigs and dried grasses.

Little Beaver raced up to Jack and pulled him to his feet. "Papa says we are to go off and play until your new house is finished!" he announced excitedly.

Meekly, Jack followed. All day long, Jack and Little Beaver played together. Before sundown they returned, and Little Beaver and Jack walked inside Jack's new house. The Duck Family had been busy arranging the cozy rooms with downy cushions and chairs, but Sadie Spider was still working on the new curtains.

Jack went outside to see his friends, who were still all there to greet him.

He was so grateful and surprised that he didn't know what to say. "Thank you very much," he finally managed.

Mr. Beaver grinned widely, displaying his gleaming white teeth. "No, Jack. Thank *you!* You are always ready to help all of us, so we wanted to do something to help you. You are a very good friend."

All during that long, cold winter, Jack had many visitors in his cozy house. There were his friends from the forest. There were his friends from the burrow. And no matter how many visitors came, there always seemed to be plenty of room for them at Jack's table.